The Lonely Sugar Plum

Deb Cerio

Published by 30th St Press

ISBN 978-1-7342660-3-0

Story and Illustrations by Debra Cerio
Design by: Peggy Sands, Indigo Disegno

I'd like to dedicate this to all the children
— the reason this book was written.
And to the big kids who contributed to its success
— primarily the members of the Chopping Block Crew
(CBC) in Boulder, CO. A long time writing group
that has been steadfast in their devotion.

And to Boulder Media Women (BMW) – who has been
an invaluable resource

And of course – to the readers – you make it real.

This is a story about
a sugar plum named Ted.
He lives in a very special place
called Sugarville.
It's only a few hops and skips
from Chistmastown.

Throughout the year,
the residents of Sugarville prepare
for December, the most joyous
month of the year.

All of the different candies are
made extra sweet. The elves keep busy
shining the lights and ornaments.
Cookies of all shapes and sizes are
baked and shipped.
(It's very important to mix
the proper amount of powdered
sugar in every batch.)

And the sugar plums
practice their magical dance
until they get it just right.

Ted is one of the sugar plums.
He is very plump and very purple.
He has beautiful sparkles that gleam
and shine as he twirls and swirls
in the sugar plum dance.

(Ted thinks they need sunglasses
but the costume director isn't
going for it.)

Unfortunately, there is a problem.
Ted is lonely. And even though
Ted is one of the best twirlers and one
of the most beautiful swirlers,
he does not know it.

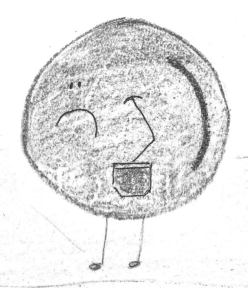

After rehearsal one day, Ted
was walking down Sugarlane when
he passed Carl the Candy cane.

"Why Carl, you have the most
beautiful candied stripes there has
ever been on a Christmas cane."

Carl got a warm feeling all over
that made him even sweeter
than he was before.

A little farther along
the lane he passed by Burt,
the stuffed Teddy bear.

"My Burt, you have the biggest,
most bestest, fluffiest paws I have
ever seen on a bear!"

"Why thank you, Ted. How nice
of you to say so."

Burt's heart sang as he waved
a big paw in Ted's direction. Ted had already
passed him. (Ted 's a very fast walker.)

Just as Ted turned the corner,
he bumped into Olive the ornament.
She was lovely!

"My Olive, how you sparkle
and shine! You will be the loveliest of all
the ornaments on the tree this year."

Olive was so happy with what
Ted had said that all she could do
was smile. He had tickled her
tongue tied!

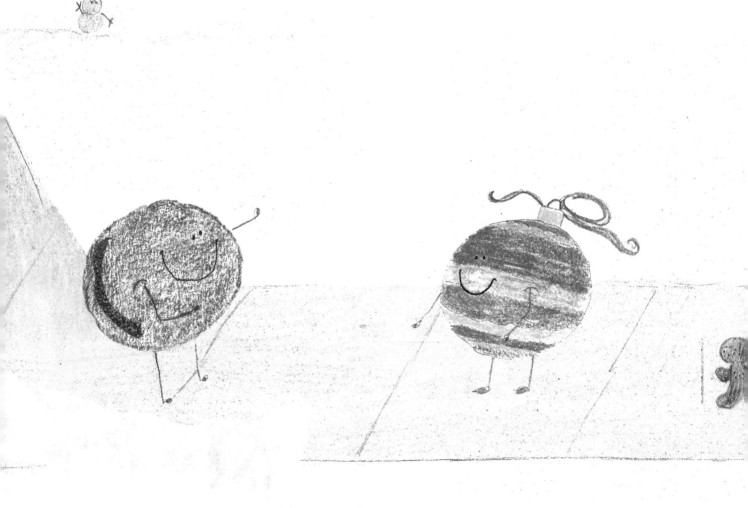

As Ted grew closer to his
little cottage, he noticed all of his
fellow villagers in their homes
drinking hot chocolate,
celebrating the spirit of the holiday
season and sharing time
with one another.

Ted felt even lonelier than
he had before. He walked a little
slower, his head drooped a little bit
lower and with a big sigh,
he shivered in the cold.

Ted knew he was supposed to be
plump, but he felt pudgy. He knew he
was supposed to be purple,
but he longed to have beautiful white
and red stripes like Carl.
His hands and feet were perfect
for sugar plum dancing, but he
wanted to have fluffy paws like Burt.

He thought if he were
as beautiful as his friends, they
would want to spend
time with him too.

Ted's

A big purple tear rolled down
his cheek and landed with a splat on
the sidewalk. It was so perfect and so
beautiful that its reflection from
the ice caught the attention
of The Snowflake Princess.
She looked through the snowball
she used to watch over the villagers.

She smiled when she saw him.
He was kind to everyone and had
spread so much goodness and cheer.
Not to mention all the sugar plums
he helps at rehearsal!

We all know that while children
sleep, visions of sugar plums dance
in their heads. (Ted is always the best
one, even with the tricky parts.)

The Princess blew
her magic snow-flake kisses.

They drifted softly throughout the village. The biggest flake landed right on top of Ted's big purple head.

In that moment, Ted realized… that the beauty he saw in others

was something he had inside himself!

Ted ran all the way back
to the center of town.
He bumped into his three friends,
Carl, Burt and Olive.
All at once, they thanked Ted for
how good he always made them feel.
They also commented on his
new dance steps and how flashy
he was at rehearsal.

"My how you twirl!" Burt said.

"No wonder the children sleep
so peacefully with visions
of you dancing in
their heads," Carl said.

Ted stood there and beamed
from cheek to cheek. His friends
thought he was beautiful too.

Just as the friends turned to
go home and get ready for the next
day's holiday festival, Olive turned
to Ted and said,

"Hey you plump purple plum,
how about joining me in my cottage
for some eggnog?"

Olive made the best eggnog within
seven counties. (Extra rum.)

He was so excited!

Ted the lonely sugar plum
wasn't lonely anymore. He was happy.

Ted realized that how you feel
about yourself is the most important
thing in the whole world.

From that moment on,
whenever Ted danced in childrens'
dreams, he always made sure to
sprinkle them with the magic kisses
the Snowflake Princess had blown
to him on that special day.
(He was very careful not to
let any slip out of his plum pockets.)

That way, every child would
know within themselves, how
very special they are.

Each and every one, just like you.

CPSIA information can be obtained
at www.ICGtesting.com
Printed in the USA
BVHW061122170821
614611BV00009B/1150